AF260996

STORIES OF SIEGFRIED

TOLD TO THE CHILDREN

BY

MARY MACGREGOR

WITH PICTURES BY
GRANVILLE FELL

Sandycroft Publishing

STORIES OF SIEGFRIED
TOLD TO THE CHILDREN

BY MARY MACGREGOR
ILLUSTRATED BY GRANVILLE FELL

First published 1909

Sandycroft Publishing
sandycroftpublishing.com

ISBN 9781492882473

Contents

List of Original Illustrations

To Denis

Dear Denis,—Here is a story that I found in an old German poem called the Nibelungenlied. The poem is full of strange adventure, adventure of both tiny dwarf and stalwart mortal.

Some of these adventures will fill this little book, and already I can see you sitting in the nursery as you read them. The door is opened but you do not look up. 'Denis! Denis!'

You are called, but you do not hear, for you are not really in the nursery any longer.

You have wandered away to Nibelheim, the home of the strange little people of whom you are reading, and you have ears only for the harsh voices of the tiny Nibelungs, eyes only for their odd, wrinkled faces.

Siegfried is the merry hero of the Nibelungenlied. I wonder will you think him as brave as French Roland or as chivalrous as your English favourite, Guy of Warwick?

Yet even should you think the German hero brave and chivalrous as these, I can hardly believe you will read and re-read this little book as often as you read and re-read the volumes which told you about your French and English heroes.

—Yours affectionately, Mary MacGregor

Mimer saw the bear

CHAPTER I
MIMER THE BLACKSMITH

Siegfried was born a Prince and grew to be a hero, a hero with a heart of gold. Though he could fight, and was as strong as any lion, yet he could love too and be as gentle as a child.

The father and mother of the hero-boy lived in a strong castle near the banks of the great Rhine river. Siegmund, his father, was a rich king, Sieglinde, his mother, a beautiful queen, and dearly did they love their little son Siegfried.

The courtiers and the high-born maidens who dwelt in the castle honoured the little Prince, and thought him the fairest child in all the land, as indeed he was.

Sieglinde, his queen-mother, would ofttimes dress her little son in costly garments and lead him by the hand before the proud, strong men-at-arms who stood before the castle walls. Nought had they but smiles and gentle words for their little Prince.

When he grew older, Siegfried would ride into the country, yet always would he be attended by King Siegmund's most trusted warriors.

Then one day armed men entered the Netherlands, the country over which King Siegmund ruled, and the little Prince was sent away from the castle, lest by any evil chance he should fall into the hands of the foe.

Siegfried was hidden away safe in the thickets of a great forest, and dwelt there under the care of a blacksmith, named Mimer.

Mimer was a dwarf, belonging to a strange race of little folk called Nibelungs. The Nibelungs lived for the most part in a dark little town beneath the ground. Nibelheim was the name of this little town and many of the tiny men who dwelt there were smiths. All the livelong day they would hammer on their little anvils, but all through the long night they would dance and play with tiny little Nibelung women.

It was not in the little dark town of Nibelheim that Mimer had his forge, but under the trees of the great forest to which Siegfried had been sent.

As Mimer or his pupils wielded their tools the wild beasts would start from their lair, and the swift birds would wing their flight through the mazes of the wood, lest danger lay in those heavy, resounding strokes.

But Siegfried, the hero-boy, would laugh for glee, and seizing the heaviest hammer he could see he would swing it with such force upon the anvil that it would be splintered into a thousand pieces.

Then Mimer the blacksmith would scold the lad, who was now the strongest of all the lads under his care; but little heeding his rebukes, Siegfried would fling himself merrily out of the smithy and hasten with great strides into the gladsome wood. For now the Prince was growing a big lad, and his strength was even as the strength of ten.

Today Siegfried was in a merry mood. He would repay Mimer's rebukes in right good fashion. He would frighten the little blacksmith dwarf until he was forced to cry for mercy.

Clad in his forest dress of deerskins, with his hair as burnished gold blowing around his shoulders, Siegfried wandered away into the depths of the woodland.

There he seized the silver horn which hung from his girdle and raised it to his lips. A long, clear note he blew, and ere the sound had died away the boy saw a sight which pleased him well.

Here was good prey indeed! A bear, a great big shaggy bear was peering at him out of a bush, and as he gazed the beast opened its jaws and growled, a fierce and angry growl. Not a whit afraid was Siegfried. Quick as lightning he had caught the great creature in his arms, and ere it could turn upon him, it was muzzled, and was being led quietly along toward the smithy.

Mimer was busy at his forge sharpening a sword when Siegfried reached the doorway.

At the sound of laughter the little dwarf raised his head. It was the Prince who laughed. Then Mimer saw the bear, and letting the sword he held drop to the ground with a clang, he ran to hide himself in the darkest corner of the smithy.

Then Siegfried laughed again. He was no hero-boy today, for next he made the big bear hunt the little Nibelung dwarf from corner to corner, nor could the frightened little man escape or hide himself in darkness. Again and again as he crouched in a shadowed corner, Siegfried would stir up the embers of the forge until all the smithy was lighted with a ruddy glow.

At length the Prince tired of his game, and unmuzzling the bear he chased the bewildered beast back into the shelter of the woodlands.

Mimer, poor little dwarf, all a-tremble with his fear, cried angrily, 'Thou mayest go shoot if so it please thee, and bring home thy dead prey. Dead bears thou mayest bring hither if thou wilt, but live bears shalt thou leave to crouch in their lair or to roam through the forest.' But Siegfried, the naughty Prince, only laughed at the little Nibelung's frightened face and harsh, croaking voice.

Now as the days passed, Mimer the blacksmith began to wish that Siegfried had never come to dwell with him in his smithy. The Prince was growing too strong, too brave to please the little dwarf, moreover many were the mischievous tricks his pupil played on him.

Prince though he was, Mimer would see if he could not get rid of his tormentor. For indeed though, as I have told you, Siegfried had a heart of gold, at this time the gold seemed to have grown dim and tarnished. Perhaps that was because the Prince had learned to distrust and to dislike, nay, more, to hate the little, cunning dwarf.

However that may be, it is certain that Siegfried played many pranks upon the little Nibelung, and he, Mimer, determined to get rid of the quick-tempered, strong-handed Prince.

One day, therefore, it happened that the little dwarf told Siegfried to go deep into the forest to bring home charcoal for the forge. And this Mimer did, though he knew that in the very part of the forest to which he was sending the lad there dwelt a terrible dragon, named Regin.

Indeed Regin was a brother of the little blacksmith, and would be lying in wait for the Prince. It would be but the work of a moment for the monster to seize the lad and greedily to devour him.

To Siegfried it was always joy to wander afar through the woodland. Ofttimes had he thrown himself down on the soft, moss-covered ground and lain there hour after hour, listening to the woodbirds' song. Sometimes he would even find a reed and try to pipe a tune as sweet as did the birds, but that was all in vain, as the lad soon found. No tiny songster would linger to hearken to the shrill piping of his grassy reed, and the Prince himself was soon ready to fling it far away.

It was no hardship then to Siegfried to leave the forge and the hated little Nibelung, therefore it was that with right goodwill he set out in search of charcoal for Mimer the blacksmith.

As he loitered there where the trees grew thickest, Siegfried took his horn and blew it lustily. If he could not pipe on a grassy reed, at least he could blow a rousing note on his silver horn.

Suddenly as Siegfried blew, the trees seemed to sway, the earth to give out fire. Regin, the dragon, had roused himself at the blast, and was even now drawing near to the Prince.

It was at the mighty strides of the monster that the trees had seemed to tremble, it was as he opened his terrible jaws that the earth had seemed to belch out fire.

For a little while Siegfried watched the dragon in silence. Then he laughed aloud, and a brave, gay laugh it was. Alone in the forest, with a sword buckled to his side, the hero was afraid of naught, not even of Regin.

The ugly monster was sitting now on a little hillock, looking down upon the lad, his victim as he thought.

Siegfried and the dragon

Then Siegfried called boldly to the dragon, 'I will kill thee, for in truth thou art an ugly monster.'

At those words Regin opened his great jaws, and showed his terrible fangs. Yet still the boy Prince mocked at the hideous dragon.

And now Regin in his fury crept closer and closer to the lad, swinging his great tail, until he well-nigh swept Siegfried from his feet.

Swiftly then the Prince drew his sword, well-tempered as he knew, for had not he himself wrought it in the forge of Mimer the blacksmith? Swiftly he drew his sword, and with one bound he sprang upon the dragon's back, and as he reared himself, down came the hero's shining sword and pierced into the very heart of the monster. Thus as Siegfried leaped nimbly to the ground, the dragon fell back dead. Regin was no longer to be feared.

Then Siegfried did a curious thing. He had heard the little Nibelung men who came to the smithy to talk with Mimer, he had heard them say that whoever should bathe in the blood of Regin the dragon would henceforth be safe from every foe. For his skin would grow so tough and horny that it would be to him as an armour through which no sword or spear could ever pierce.

Thinking of the little Nibelungs' harsh voices and wrinkled little faces, as they had sat talking thus around Mimer's glowing forge, Siegfried now flung aside his deerskin dress and bathed himself from top to toe in the dragon's blood.

But as he bathed, a leaf from off a linden tree was blown upon his shoulders, and on the spot where it rested Siegfried's skin was still soft and tender as when he was a little child. It was only a tiny spot which was covered by the linden leaf, but should a spear thrust, or an arrow pierce that tiny spot, Siegfried would be wounded as easily as any other man.

The dragon was dead, the bath was over, and clad once more in his deerskin, Siegfried set out for the smithy. He brought no charcoal for the forge; all that he carried with him was a heart afire with anger, a sword quivering to take the life of the Nibelung, Mimer.

For now Siegfried knew that the dwarf had wished to send him forth to death, when he bade him go seek charcoal in the depths of the forest.

Into the dusky glow of the smithy plunged the hero, and swiftly he slew the traitor Mimer. Then gaily, for he had but slain evil ones of whom the world was well rid, then gaily Siegfried fared through the forest in quest of adventure.

CHAPTER II
SIEGFRIED WINS THE TREASURE

Now this is what befell the Prince. In his wanderings he reached the country called Isenland, where the warlike but beautiful Queen Brunhild reigned. He gazed with

wonder at her castle, so strong it stood on the edge of the sea, guarded by seven great gates. Her marble palaces also made him marvel, so white they glittered in the sun.

But most of all he marvelled at this haughty queen, who refused to marry any knight unless he could vanquish her in every contest to which she summoned him.

Brunhild from the castle window saw the fair face and the strong limbs of the hero, and demanded that he should be brought into her presence, and as a sign of her favour she showed the young Prince her magic horse Gana.

Yet Siegfried had no wish to conquer the warrior-queen and gain her hand and her broad dominions for his own. Siegfried thought only of a wonder-maiden, unknown, unseen as yet, though in his heart he hid an image of her as he dreamed that she would be.

It is true that Siegfried had no love for the haughty Brunhild. It is also true that he wished to prove to her that he alone was a match for all her boldest warriors, and had even power to bewitch her magic steed, Gana, if so he willed, and steal it from her side.

And so one day a spirit of mischief urged the Prince on to a gay prank, as also a wayward spirit urged him no longer to brook Queen Brunhild's haughty mien.

Before he left Isenland, therefore, Siegfried in a merry mood threw to the ground the seven great gates that guarded the Queen's strong castle. Then he called to Gana, the magic steed, to follow him into the world, and this the charger did with right goodwill. Whether Siegfried sent Gana back to Isenland or not I do not know, but I know that in the days to come Queen Brunhild never forgave the hero for his daring feat.

When the Prince had left Isenland he rode on and on until he came to a great mountain. Here near a cave he found two little dwarfish Nibelungs, surrounded by twelve foolish giants. The two little Nibelungs were princes, the giants were their counsellors.

Now the King of the Nibelungs had but just died in the dark little underground town of Nibelheim, and the two tiny princes were the sons of the dead king.

But they had not come to the mountainside to mourn for their royal father. Not so indeed had they come, but to divide the great hoard of treasure which the King had bequeathed to them at his death.

Already they had begun to quarrel over the treasure, and the twelve foolish giants looked on, but did not know what to say or do, so they did nothing, and never spoke at all.

The dwarfs had themselves carried the hoard out of the cave where usually it was hidden, and they had spread it on the mountainside.

There it lay, gold as far as the eye could see, and farther. Jewels, too, were there, more than twelve wagons could carry away in four days and nights, each going three journeys.

Indeed, however much you took from this marvellous treasure, never did it seem to grow less. But more precious even than the gold or the jewels of the hoard was a wonderful sword which it possessed. It was named Balmung, and had been tempered by the Nibelungs in their glowing forges underneath the glad green earth.

Before the magic strength of Balmung's stroke, the strongest warrior must fall, nor could his armour save him, however close its links had been welded by some doughty smith. As Siegfried rode towards the two little dwarfs, they turned and saw him, with his bright, fair face, and flowing locks.

Magic sword

Nimble as little hares they darted to his side, and begged that he would come and divide their treasure. He should have the good sword Balmung as reward, they cried.

Siegfried dismounted, well pleased to do these ugly little men a kindness.

But alas! ere long the dwarfs began to mock at the hero with their harsh voices, and to wag their horrid little heads at him, while they screamed in a fury that he was not dividing the treasure as they wished.

Then Siegfried grew angry with the tiny princes, and seizing the magic sword, he cut off their heads. The twelve foolish giants also he slew, and thus became himself master of the marvellous hoard as well as of the good sword Balmung.

Seven hundred valiant champions, hearing the blast of the hero's horn, now gathered together to defend the country from this strange young warrior. But he vanquished them all, and forced them to promise that they would henceforth serve no other lord save him alone. And this they did, being proud of his great might.

Now tidings of the slaughter of the two tiny princes had reached Nibelheim, and great was the wrath of the little men and little women who dwelt in the dark town beneath the earth.

Alberich, the mightiest of all the dwarfs, gathered together his army of little gnomes to avenge the death of the two dwarf princes and also, for Alberich was a greedy man, to gain for himself the great hoard.

When Siegfried saw Alberich at the head of his army of little men he laughed aloud, and with a light heart he chased them all into the great cave on the mountainside.

From off the mighty dwarf, Alberich, he stripped his famous Cloak of Darkness, which made him who wore it not only invisible, but strong as twelve strong men. He snatched also from the dwarf's fingers his wishing rod, which was a Magic Wand. And last of all he made Alberich and his thousands of tiny warriors take an oath, binding them evermore to serve him alone.

Then hiding the treasure in the cave with the seven hundred champions whom he had conquered, he left Alberich and his army of little men to guard it, until he came again.

And Alberich and his dwarfs were faithful to the hero who had shorn them of their treasure, and served him for evermore.

Siegfried, the magic sword Balmung by his side, the Cloak of Darkness thrown over his arm, the Magic Wand in his strong right hand, went over the mountain, across the plains, nor did he tarry until he came again to the castle built on the banks of the river Rhine in his own low-lying country of the Netherlands.

CHAPTER III
SIEGFRIED COMES HOME

The walls of the old castle rang. King Siegmund, his knights and liegemen, all were welcoming Prince Siegfried home. They had not seen their hero-prince

since he had been sent long years before to be under the charge of Mimer the blacksmith.

He had grown but more fair, more noble, they thought, as they gazed upon his stalwart limbs, his fearless eyes.

And what tales of prowess clustered around his name! Already their Prince had done great deeds as he had ridden from land to land.

The King and his liegemen had heard of the slaughter of the terrible dragon, of the capture of the great treasure, of the defiance of the warlike and beautiful Brunhild. They could wish for no more renowned prince than their own Prince Siegfried.

Thus Siegmund and his subjects rejoiced that the heir to the throne was once again in his own country.

In the Queen's bower, too, there was great joy. Sieglinde wept, but her tears were not those of sadness. Sieglinde wept for very gladness that her son had come home safe from his wonderful adventures.

Now Siegmund wished to give a great feast in honour of his son. It should be on his birthday which was very near, the birthday on which the young Prince would be twenty-one years of age.

Far and wide throughout the Netherlands and into distant realms tidings of the feast were borne. Kinsmen and strangers, lords and ladies all were asked to the banquet in the great castle hall where Siegmund reigned supreme.

Siegmund the king

It was the merry month of June when the feast was held, and the sun shone bright on maidens in fair raiment, on knights in burnished armour.

Siegfried was to be knighted on this June day along with four hundred young squires of his father's realm. The Prince was clad in gorgeous armour, and on the cloak flung around his shoulders jewels were seen to sparkle in the sunlight, jewels made fast with gold embroidery worked by the white hands of the Queen and her fair damsels.

In games and merry pastimes the hours of the day sped fast away, until the great bell of the Minster pealed, calling the gay company to the house of God for evensong.

Siegfried and the four hundred squires knelt before the altar, ere they were knighted by the royal hand of Siegmund the King. The solemn service ended, the new-made knights hastened back to the castle, and there in the great hall a mighty tournament was held. Knights who had grown grey in service tilted with those who but that day had been given the grace of knighthood. Lances splintered, shields fell before the mighty onslaughts of the gallant warriors, until King Siegmund bade the tilting cease.

Then in the great hall feasting and song held sway until daylight faded and the stars shone bright.

Yet no weariness knew the merrymakers. The next morning, and for six long summer days, they tilted, they sang, they feasted.

When at length the great festival drew to a close, Siegmund in the presence of his guests gave to his dear son Siegfried many lands and strong castles over which he might be lord.

To all his son's comrades, too, the King gave steeds and costly raiment, while Queen Sieglinde bestowed upon them freely coins of gold. Such abundant gifts had never before been dreamed of as were thus lavished by Siegmund and Sieglinde on their guests.

As the rich nobles looked upon the brave young Prince Siegfried, there were some who whispered among themselves that they would fain have him to rule in the land.

Siegfried heard their whispers, but in no wise did he give heed to the wish of the nobles.

Never, he thought, while his beautiful mother and his bounteous father lived, would he wear the crown.

Indeed Siegfried had no wish to sit upon a throne, he wished but to subdue the evildoers in the land. Or better still he wished to go forth in search of new adventure. And this right soon he did.

CHAPTER IV
KRIEMHILD'S DREAM

Now in the Kingdom of Burgundy the court sat in the city of Worms, a city built on the banks of the great Rhine river.

At this court dwelt a beautiful Princess named Kriemhild. More beautiful was she than any other maiden in the wide world. Gentle and kind too she was, so that her fame had spread to many a far-off land.

The King, her father, had died when Kriemhild was a tiny maiden. Her mother was Queen Uté, who loved well her beautiful and gentle daughter.

But though the maiden's father was dead, she was well guarded by her three royal brothers, King Gunther, King Gernot, and King Giselher.

It was King Gunther, Kriemhild's eldest brother, who sat upon the throne, and it was to him that the liegemen took their oath of fealty.

King Gunther's chief counsellor was his uncle, a cruel man, whose name was Hagen.

There was great wealth and splendour at the Court of Worms, and many nobles and barons flocked thither to take service under King Gunther's banners.

Now one night it chanced that Kriemhild dreamed a strange dream. As she lay in her soft, white bed it seemed to the Princess that a beautiful hawk, with feathers of gold, came and perched upon her wrist.

Strong and wild was the bird, but in her dream Kriemhild fondled and petted it until it grew quiet and tame. Then the Princess dressed herself for the hunt, and with her hawk on her wrist set out with her three royal brothers to enjoy the sport. No sooner, however, did the maiden loosen the hawk from off her wrist than it soared upward toward the bright blue sky.

Then the dream-maiden saw two mighty eagles swoop down upon her petted hawk, and bearing it away in their cruel talons, tear it into pieces.

When the Princess awoke and remembered her dream she trembled for fear. In the early dawn the beautiful maiden slipped into her mother's bower. Perchance the Queen would be able to tell her the meaning of her dream.

Queen Uté listened kindly to her daughter's fears, but when she heard of the two cruel eagles she covered her face with her fair white hands and answered slowly: 'The hawk, my daughter, is a noble knight who shall be thy husband, but, alas, unless God defend him from his foes, thou shalt lose him ere he has long been thine.'

But the beautiful maiden tossed her head, forgetting the sorrow of her dream, and cried with a light heart, 'O lady mother, I wish no knight to woo me from thy side. Merry and glad is my life here in our court at Worms, and here will I dwell with thee and my three royal brothers.'

'Nay,' said the Queen, 'speak not thus, fair daughter, for God will send to thee a noble knight and strong.'

Yet still the maiden laughed. She knew not that even now a hero of great renown was on his way to the royal city, a hero who already bore the maiden's image in his heart, and hoped to win her one day for his bride.

CHAPTER V
SIEGFRIED JOURNEYS TO WORMS

The Netherlands, as to many another land, came rumours of the beauty and the gentleness of the Princess Kriemhild. Siegfried at first paid little heed to what he

heard of a wonder-maid who dwelt in the famous court of Worms. Yet by and by he began to think she was strangely like the unknown maid whose image he carried in his heart.

When he heard that many knights had ridden far that they might see this fair Princess, he made up his mind that he also would go thither to the court at Worms.

Siegmund and Sieglinde had often begged the Prince to wed some great princess. He thought, therefore, that they would be well pleased that he was going into Burgundy to see the beautiful maiden Kriemhild.

But the King and Queen were grieved when they knew that Siegfried must leave them. Kriemhild, it was true, was as good as she was beautiful, but two of her brothers were proud and haughty men of Burgundy, moreover their uncle Hagen had a grim and cruel temper, and it was he who really ruled the land. It might be that their son would not be welcomed to the court at Worms, and ill might betide him in a strange country.

Yet Siegfried would have his way. He must certainly go to Burgundy to woo the gentle maiden who had already sent many knights away, unmoved by all their vows of courtesy and love. For, indeed, no knight yet had the lady seen whom she would call her lord.

Then Siegmund, seeing that Siegfried had determined to go to Worms, warned him that King Gunther was too weak to be trusted, while Hagen his chief counsellor was so powerful at court that he might work ill on whom he would. As of old, the hero laughed aloud.

'Should Hagen deny what I shall ask in courtesy, he shall learn that strong is my right hand!' cried the Prince. 'His country and his kings I will surely wrest from him if he treat me with disdain.'

'Speak not thus foolishly,' said King Siegmund. 'Should thy wild words be carried to Hagen's ears, thou wouldst never be allowed to cross the borders of his country. If go thou must to Burgundy, take with thee an armed force. See, I will summon my warriors to follow thee lest danger befall.'

'Nay, but an army will I not take with me, lest Gunther dream I have come to invade his land. I, with eleven brave knights to follow me, will ride to Burgundy. Your help do I crave, good father. Give me, I pray thee, eleven stalwart warriors.'

Then Siegmund called for eleven of his bravest knights, and bade them prepare to follow their Prince.

Meanwhile Queen Sieglinde had been weeping bitterly for fear lest her dear son should fall into danger in King Gunther's country.

But Siegfried stole to her side, and taking her frail, white hands in his strong ones, he said tenderly, 'Lady mother, I pray thee weep not, neither fear for me.' Then, knowing well what would please the Queen best, he pleaded with her to aid him in his adventure.

'Provide me and my eleven knights with beautiful garments,' thus he coaxed his lady mother, 'that we may go to Burgundy clad as proud heroes should.'

Swiftly the Queen dried her tears. 'If go thou must, dear son,' she said, 'thou shalt go clothed in the best apparel ever warrior wore, thou and also thy brave comrades.'

Thus day by day, while the eleven warriors polished their armour until it shone as the noontide sun, Sieglinde and her maidens sat stitching, stitching. Gladly they stitched, nor ever did their fingers loiter at their seams until Prince Siegfried's garments were complete.

At length all was ready and Siegfried and his eleven brave warriors took farewell of their native land. Gently the bold hero kissed his lady mother as once again her sad tears fell. 'Fear not, dear mother,' he said, 'fear not; ere long I will return and bring with me the beauteous maiden Kriemhild.' Yet the Queen and her maidens wept, and over the little band of knights a sudden gloom fell, they knew not why.

But ere long as they journeyed along, gay thoughts cheered the warriors, laughter and merry jests filled the air, for were they not going forward to fame and fair adventure.

For six days Siegfried and his knights journeyed, and on the seventh they reached the sandbank by the Rhine which led them into Worms. Boldly, and clad in their most costly garments, the Prince and his companions entered the royal city.

Siegfried enters Worms

CHAPTER VI
SIEGFRIED'S WELCOME TO WORMS

As the heroes entered the streets of Worms the people came out of their houses all agape with wonder. Who could the bold strangers be? See how their horses' trappings shone as burnished gold and how their white armour glittered in the sunlight.

Then down from the castle rode Gunther's warriors to welcome the strangers. Right courteously did they greet Siegfried and his eleven brave knights. As the custom was, they sent their minions to lead away the strangers' chargers to the stalls, and to bear their shields to a place of safety.

But Siegfried cried gaily, 'Nay, from our steeds and our armour will we not part, for ere long I and my gallant warriors will ride away again to our own country. I pray thee now tell me where I shall find thy King, for to speak with him came I thither.'

'King Gunther,' cried his warriors, 'is even now seated in yonder hall, and around him are gathered many gallant heroes, many brave knights.'

Now in the hall tidings had reached King Gunther of the band of strangers who had so boldly entered into the royal city.

When he heard of their gorgeous raiment and their shining armour, much did he desire to know from whence they came.

Then one of his lords said to the King, 'We know not who these strangers be, yet if thou wilt send for Hagen, it may be he can tell thee. For to Hagen strange lands are well known, as also the kings and princes who dwell therein.'

Therefore Hagen was summoned in all haste to the presence of King Gunther. 'Tell me now,' said the King, as his counsellor bowed low before him, 'tell me, if in truth thou knowest, who be these strangers that ride so boldly towards the castle?'

Strong and stern Hagen stood up before the King. No winsome hero was this man, but a warrior fierce and grim, with eyes to pierce all on whom he gazed, so keen, so quick they were.

'The truth, sire, will I tell to thee,' answered Hagen, and he walked over to the castle window, flung it wide and cast his searching glance on Siegfried and his noble knights, who were now drawing near to the castle.

Well was the grim counsellor pleased with the splendour of these strangers with their shining helmets, their dazzling white armour, their noble chargers, yet from whence they came he could not tell.

Hagen turned from the window to where the King stood awaiting his answer.

'Whence come these knights I know not,' he said. 'Yet so noble is their bearing that they must needs be princes or ambassadors from some great monarch. One knight, the fairest and the boldest, is, methinks, the wondrous hero Siegfried, though never have I seen that mighty Prince.'

Then, his fierce eyes gleaming, Hagen told the King of the great treasure Siegfried had won from the Nibelungs. His eyes gleamed with a greed he could not hide as he told King Gunther of the gold that had been strewed upon the mountainside, of the jewels that had sparkled there, for Hagen was envious of the riches of the great hero.

He told the King, too, how Siegfried had seized the good sword Balmung, and with it had killed the two little princely dwarfs, their twelve giants and seven hundred great champions of the neighbouring country. Of Alberich, too, Hagen told his master, of Alberich from whom Siegfried had taken the Cloak of Darkness and the Magic Wand, and who now guarded the hoard for the mighty hero alone.

Never was such a warrior as Siegfried, thought King Gunther, who was himself neither strong nor brave.

But yet more had Hagen to tell, even how Siegfried had slain a great dragon and bathed in its blood until his skin grew tough and horny, so that no sword-thrust could do him any hurt.

But of the linden leaf and of the tiny spot between the hero's shoulders where he could be smitten as easily as any other knight, of these things Hagen, knowing nothing, did not speak.

'Let us hasten to receive this young Prince,' said the counsellor, 'as befits his fame. Let us hasten to gain his goodwill lest our country suffer from his prowess.'

The King was well pleased with the counsel of his uncle Hagen, for as he gazed at the young hero from the castle window King Gunther loved him for his strength of limb, for his fair young face, and would fain welcome him to the land of Burgundy.

'If in truth the knight be Siegfried,' said the King, 'right glad am I. More bold and peerless a prince have I never seen.'

'Siegfried, if so he be, is the son of a wealthy king,' said Hagen. 'Well pleased would I be to know for what purpose he and his knights have journeyed to our land.'

'Let us go down and welcome the strangers,' said Gunther. 'If their errand be peaceful they shall tarry at our court and see how merry the knights of Burgundy can be.'

With Hagen by his side and followed by his courtiers, Gunther then walked toward the gates of the castle, which he reached as Siegfried and his knights rode through them.

Graciously then did the King welcome the noble knight, and Siegfried, bowing low, thanked him for his kindly greeting.

'I beseech thee, noble knight,' said the King, 'tell me why thou hast journeyed to this our royal city, for thy purpose is yet unknown.'

Now Siegfried was not ready to speak of the fair Princess of whom he had heard in his own country, so he answered the King thus:

'Tidings reached me in my fatherland of the splendour of thy court, O King. Never monarch was more bold, more brave than thou, never ruler had more valiant warriors. Such tales were told to me by the people of my land and I have come to see if they be true. I also, King Gunther, am a warrior, and I, too, shall one day wear a crown, for I am Siegfried, Prince of the Netherlands.

Nor shall I be content until I have done great deeds to make the whole world marvel. For then in truth will people cry aloud that I am worthy to reign.'

At that moment Siegfried caught sight of Hagen's grim, stern face, and something he saw in it provoked the gay prince to say right hardily, 'Therefore to do great deeds have I come to Worms, even to wrest from thee, King Gunther, thy broad realm of Burgundy and likewise all thy castles. They shall be mine ere many suns have set.'

Then indeed did the King and all his warriors marvel at the bold young knight. 'Was ever heard so monstrous a plan?' murmured the warriors each to the other. 'The stripling from a foreign land, with but eleven bold knights to aid him, would seize Burgundy and banish the King from his realm. It is a monstrous plan.'

'Thou dost repay my welcome but coldly,' said Gunther to the valorous knight 'My fathers ruled over these lands; with honour did they rule. Wherefore then shall they be taken from their son?'

But Siegfried cried, 'Thyself must fight and win peace for thy fatherland. For unless thou dost conquer me I shall rule in my great might in this realm, and when I die it shall be my heir who shall become king.'

Then Gunther's brother, King Gernot, spoke, and peaceful were his words.

'We rule over a fair country, bold knight, and our liegemen serve us in all good faith. No need have we to fight for this our fatherland. Therefore do thou go and leave us in peace.'

But King Gunther's warriors listened sullenly to the words of Gernot, and they muttered, 'Such words shall scarce save the braggart stranger, for hath he not challenged our King to fight,' and the hands of the stout warriors crept to their sword-hilts. 'We will master this haughty Prince,' they cried aloud then in their anger.

Hot was Siegfried's temper as he heard their words, and proudly did he answer, 'Ye are all but vassals and would ye measure swords with me, a king's son? Nor, should ye fall on me altogether, could ye hope to overcome me,' and Siegfried swung aloft his good sword Balmung. Then one of the stout warriors whom

Siegfried thus defied called lustily for his armour and his shield.

But again King Gernot spoke. 'Not yet hath Siegfried done us any hurt, let us not provoke him to fierce deeds, rather let us seek to gain his goodwill.'

King Gunther looked at Hagen. He was not content that his chief counsellor should keep silence. And indeed at that very moment Hagen's stern voice was heard.

'We do well to be wrathful at the words of this bold stripling,' he said, his keen eyes glancing fiercely meanwhile at Gernot. 'We do well to be wrathful, for why should Siegfried thus mock at us who have never done him aught of ill?'

'Dost think I but mock thee with my words,' cried the rash knight. 'Ere long thou shalt see the deeds which my strong right hand shall do in this fair land of Burgundy.'

Again amid the angry tumult Gernot's voice was raised, forbidding his warriors to answer the stranger with harsh words.

As Gernot's peaceful voice fell upon Siegfried's ear for the third time, he began to think of Kriemhild, the wonder-lady of his dreams. He grew ashamed of his anger. He would curb it lest he should never win the Princess for his bride.

Then Gernot, seeing the fierceness die out of the stranger's face, spoke yet again. 'Thou shalt be welcome, thou and thy comrades, to Worms, and right glad will we be to serve thee,' and Gernot ordered goblets of the King's wine to be brought to the strange guests.

Siegfried and his knights took the goblets, and having drained them they were ready to forget their warlike words.

King Gunther, seeing that his guests were no longer angry, led them to the banqueting hall, and Siegfried was soon laughing his own glad, gay laugh. When at length the feast was ended the stranger knights were lodged each as befitted his rank.

Then throughout the fair land of Burgundy there stole the story of the King's bold hero guest, Sir Siegfried.

CHAPTER VII
SIEGFRIED'S SOJOURN AT WORMS

At the court of Worms high festival was held to do honour to Siegfried and his eleven brave warriors. It is true that his boldness when he entered the city had

made the Kings and their liegemen wish to serve the dauntless hero, yet now it was not of his boldness that they thought, but of his happy, winsome ways. Indeed it was but a short time until he was the most favoured Prince in all the gallant throng of courtiers that gathered round King Gunther in his royal city.

Only one in all the country hated the gallant Prince of the Netherlands, and that one was the stern and fierce-eyed Hagen; but of the counsellor's ill-will the lighthearted hero knew nought.

Merry were the frolics, gay the pastimes at the court of Worms, and in every game and sport Siegfried was the most skilful.

Did the warriors hurl the stone? None could hurl it as far as could Siegfried. Did they leap? No one ever leaped as far as did the Prince. Did they go a-hunting? No one brought down the prey as often as did the hero. Did they tilt in the tournament? Siegfried it was who ever gained the prize. Yet none was envious of the Prince, so glad he was, so light of heart.

When games were held in the great castle hall, ladies clad in garments of richest hue, and sparkling with gems of ruddy gold, would come into the galleries. And ever as they watched the gallant knights their eyes would follow the most gallant of them all, the hero Siegfried.

But among these fair counts and ladies the Princess Kriemhild was never to be seen, and Siegfried had no thought to spare for any other damsel. In his heart was ever the image of the maiden whom he had come hither to win.

The Princess might not go down to the great hall to see the tournament, yet as she sat in her tower she would ofttimes think of the mighty strength of this hero, of his heart of gold. And almost before she was aware Kriemhild had found the Prince whom she would gladly call her lord.

When she heard the knights running and leaping in the courtyard, Kriemhild would lay her seam aside, and Princess though she was, she would run to her lattice window, and peeping through, she would watch her hero with glad eyes, victor in every pastime. Nor would she turn away until the sports were ended and the courtyard once again grew silent and deserted.

Siegfried did not know that Kriemhild's glad eyes were peeping through her lattice window, and had he known he would scarce have dared to dream that her glance was fixed on no other save on him alone.

Indeed sometimes the hero's heart misgave him. When would he see the maiden whom he loved? Had she no pleasure in his knightly games, no smile to give him for his skill? Nay, she was as great a stranger to him now as when he had ridden into the royal city of Worms in hope to gain her favour.

Thus for one whole year Siegfried dwelt with the three Kings of Burgundy, and during all that time he never once saw the wonder-lady of his dreams, the Princess Kriemhild.

At the end of the year King Gunther's fair realm of Burgundy was threatened with invasion and with mighty wars. No longer did the castle hall at Worms ring with the merry pastimes of the courtiers. All was grave, silent, for King Gunther and his brothers and his counsellors were in sore distress.

That day heralds had ridden into the land and demanded audience of King Gunther.

'Now who hath sent you hither?' said the King in angry mood.

'Our masters,' cried the heralds. 'King Ludegast and King Ludeger have sent us to warn thee that they hate thee and will invade thy land. With great armies will they come to thy realm of Burgundy. Within twelve weeks will they be here, unless thou dost offer a ransom for thy kingdom.'

'Tarry a little,' said Gunther, 'until I have spoken with my counsellors, then shall ye carry my answer back to thy masters.'

King Gernot had heard the challenge of the heralds, and dauntless he cried, 'Our good swords shall defend us. What fear we from the foreign host!'

But Hagen cried, 'Ludegast and Ludeger are fierce, and evil will overtake us, for scarce have we time in which to gather our liegemen together ere the foe will be in our land. Speak thou, O King, unto the hero Siegfried. It may be that his powers can help us now.'

Meanwhile King Gunther commanded that the heralds should be lodged with all due courtesy, and this he did for the sake of his fair fame. Now as Gunther sat brooding over the evil which seemed as though it would overtake his land, Siegfried came to his side. He knew no reason for the King's distress.

'What hath come to pass,' said the hero, 'that all our merry pastimes are ended? For since ever I came into the fair land of Burgundy hath the castle hall of thy royal city echoed with the ring of knightly deeds, and tilts and jousts have long held sway. Why, therefore, are the merry pastimes ended, and wherefore dost thou sit here thus sad and downcast?'

'Not to everyone,' said King Gunther, 'would I tell my sorrow, nay, to none save a steadfast friend dare I declare it.'

When Siegfried heard the King's words, his fair face flushed, then paled again.

'Already,' cried the hero, 'have I followed thee in time of need. For indeed during the year which he had spent at Worms, Siegfried had gone with Gunther on more than one foray into the neighbouring kingdoms.

'Now,' he continued, 'now if trouble hath come to thee my arm is strong to bring thee aid. I will be thy friend if thou art willing while life is mine.'

'God reward thee, Sir Siegfried!' cried King Gunther, and right glad of heart was he. 'It may be I shall not need thy strength to aid me in my battles, yet do I rejoice that thou art my friend. Never while my life lasts shalt thou be sorry for thy words.'

Then King Gunther told to the brave knight the insolent message which the heralds had brought from their masters, Ludegast and Ludeger.

'Thou needst not be troubled at these tidings,' said the young knight. 'If thy foes were as many as thirty thousand, yet with one thousand warriors would I destroy them. Therefore leave the battle in my hands.'

King Gunther, for he was not very brave, rejoiced at Siegfried's words, and scattered his fears to the four winds.

Then he sent for the heralds, and bade them return to their masters to say that King Gunther defied their threats, and in proof thereof would ere long send an army to punish them for their insolence.

Now when the heralds reached their own country with these tidings, King Ludegast of Denmark, and King Ludeger the Saxon, who was his brother, were filled with dread. Moreover the heralds told them that the famous hero Siegfried would fight for Burgundy, and when they heard that the hearts of the rude kings failed for fear.

In great haste they gathered together their warriors, and soon Ludegast had twenty thousand men ready to defend his land. Ludeger the Saxon, too, had called together even more than forty thousand men, and the two armies formed a mighty host.

King Gunther meanwhile had assembled his men, and the chief command was given to Hagen with the grim face and the piercing eyes. When Siegfried saw that Gunther was buckling on his armour he drew near to him, and said, 'Sir King, stay thou at home in the royal city and guard the women. Neither dost thou have any fear, for in good sooth, I can protect both thine honour and thy men.'

And King Gunther stayed in the royal city while his warriors went forth to battle.

From the Rhine river Gunther's vast army marched toward the Saxon country, and all along the borders they smote those who were in favour of their foes, until fear fell upon those lands.

Then leaving Hagen with the main army, Siegfried rode forward alone to seek the foe. Nor was it long ere on a plain before him he saw a great host encamped.

In advance of the great army of more than forty thousand men stood a single warrior, as though he were a sentinel guarding the plain.

A shining shield of gold was in his hand, and when Siegfried saw that, he knew that the sentinel was none other than Ludegast himself.

Even as Siegfried knew his enemy and spurred forward his steed, Ludegast saw the hero. Digging his spurs into the sides of his horse he also sprang forward, and, with lances poised, the two mighty men met and charged with all their strength.

On dashed the noble steeds as though driven by a tempest, until the King and the Prince drew rein, and turning faced each other once again, their swords now in their hands.

With such great strokes did Siegfried ply his foe, that fiery sparks flamed all around the helmet of the King, while the noise of his mighty blows filled the space around as with peals of thunder.

King Ludegast was a worthy foe and many an ugly thrust did Siegfried parry with his shield. But at length with his good sword Balmung, the hero pierced through the steel harness of Ludegast the King. Three times he struck, until his enemy lay helpless at his feet. With piteous moan then did Ludegast beg the Prince to spare his life, and this Siegfried did.

Then, as the hero was going to sheathe his sword, up rode thirty of the King's warriors, who had watched the fray from afar. Fiercely they beset the hero who had vanquished their King and stealthily did they seek to rescue his prisoner. But Siegfried brandished his good sword Balmung, and with his own strong right hand slaughtered the thirty warriors, all save one. Him the Prince spared that he might carry the dire tidings of the capture of King Ludegast to the army on the plain.

Then Siegfried, left alone with his royal prisoner, lifted him on to his own charger, and brought him to Hagen.

But the Prince did not linger with the army. Without delay he set out for the forefront of the fray, and close behind him rode his own eleven knights, while Gernot followed with a thousand men. And soon the great plain was a grim battlefield.

Loud and fierce was the conflict. Many a clanging blow fell upon uplifted shields, many an eager sword-thrust struck through helmet and through mail, and ever in the thickest of the fight rode Siegfried, the valiant Prince of the Netherlands.

The hero was seeking for King Ludeger, the leader of the Saxon host. Three times did he cleave his way through the mighty host until at length he stood before the King.

Now Ludeger had seen how Siegfried swung his good sword Balmung, and how he cleft in twain the helmet of many of the toughest warriors in the Saxon army, and his heart was filled with rage. He knew also that his brother Ludegast had been taken captive by this same bold Prince.

Thus it was that when Siegfried stood before his royal foe, the onslaught of the King was more violent than the hero had expected. So violent was it that the Prince's war-horse staggered and well-nigh fell.

With a mighty effort, the steed recovered from the shock, but the rage of the hero was terrible. In his eagerness to reach the fierce King Ludeger he dismounted, as also did his foe, and thus they fought, while all around them flew the splinters of broken swords and spears.

At length with a great blow Siegfried struck the shield from Ludeger's hold; a moment more and he had him at his mercy. For the second time that day the Prince was victor over a King.

As Siegfried stooped to bind his prisoner, Ludeger's eyes fell upon the crown which was emblazoned on his victor's shield. Then he knew that the rumour which had reached him was true. This mighty hero was none other than Siegfried, the son of Siegmund, King of the Netherlands.

Vain was it to fight longer with such a hero among their foes, and Ludeger raised his voice loud above the tumult, and cried to his brave Saxon warriors, 'My warriors, my lieges, cease to give battle. Lay down your arms, lower your standards, for none may conquer where Prince Siegfried wars.'

At Ludeger's words all that was left of the great armies of Danes and Saxons laid down their arms, lowered their standards, while their King humbly sued for peace.

By Hagen's command peace was granted, but Ludeger, along with Ludegast and five hundred warriors who had been taken prisoner, were forced to go with the Burgundians to the royal city of Worms.

The victorious army was soon upon its homeward way, the wounded being carried in litters by the command of King Gernot.

Tidings were sent to King Gunther, telling him to rejoice, for his warriors had won the day. Yet to all it was well known that the victory was due to the prowess of the mighty Prince Siegfried.

Nor did the heralds who were sent to the city with the glad news of victory forget to tell of the marvellous deeds of the hero.

In Worms there had been grief lest their warriors should be vanquished, but now the city was full of triumph, and noble dames and happy maidens gathered round the squires who had brought the good news.

Then Kriemhild sent secretly for one of the squires, for she wished to hear without delay all that had befallen her gallant knight. Had she not mourned his absence and scarce slept the long nights through lest danger should come nigh so fearless a warrior? Had she not vowed to herself that she would own no other knight as lord, save only this great hero?

For unawares love had stolen into the tender heart of the Lady Kriemhild.

When the squire was led to the bower of the Princess, he stood quiet, modest before the beauteous lady.

'Tell me the dear tidings,' she said, 'stint not thy words, and gold will I give to thee in plenty.'

Yet at first the Princess had no courage to ask of Siegfried's prowess.

'How fared my brother Gernot, and how have my other kinsmen fought? Are many wounded left upon the field?'

Then to her lips sprang the words she would fain have the squire answer before all others.

'And who did best of any?' said the Princess, and her voice broke, and her tears fell as she spoke.

But the young squire knew what the maiden wished to hear, and he told her of the mighty deeds done on the battlefield, and how ever in the forefront, where the danger was the greatest, was to be seen the gallant Prince of the Netherlands, his good sword Balmung in his hand.

Of his two royal captives, too, the young squire told, and as Kriemhild listened to the exploits of her knight, her lovely face became rosy red with delight.

Well rewarded indeed was the squire for his joyous tidings, for the Princess gave him costly raiment and ten gold coins as well.

Ere many more days had passed away there came the tramp of armed men along the banks of the great Rhine river. The troops were coming home.

Then to the windows of the castle rushed the maidens, and among them was the beautiful Princess, and together they watched as the warriors rode through the streets of the royal city.

King Gunther himself went forth to welcome his troops, and to thank the young hero who had so gallantly saved the realm of Burgundy from invasion.

Of all those who had gone forth to battle but sixty men were left behind, stricken by the foe.

The royal prisoners Ludegast and Ludeger the King treated with honour. He indeed promised to set them free if their liege-men, who had been taken prisoners, would stay as hostages in his land. And this the prisoners were well pleased to do, that their Kings might return without ransom to their own lands.

Siegfried the hero now began to think that it was fitting that he should go back to his old father Siegmund, and his dear mother Sieglinde.

But King Gunther, to whom he told his wish, entreated him to stay yet a little longer in the royal city.

'For now,' said the King, 'will we hold a merry festival and kings and princes will we summon to our court. Stay, then, Sir Siegfried, that thou mayest show thy skill in the great tournament.'

Yet it was neither the wishes of the King nor the thought of the tournament which made Siegfried willing to linger on still in the fair Burgundian town. It was the image of a gentle maiden, whom yet he had never seen, which kept him from speeding home to his own country.

Perchance if he waited he would see her soon, the wonder-maiden, whose image even on the battlefield was safe hidden in his heart.

CHAPTER VIII
SIEGFRIED SEES KRIEMHILD

Queen Uté, the mother of Kriemhild, heard that a great festival was to be held, and she made up her mind that she and her daughter should grace it with their presence.

Then was there great glee among the hand-maidens of the Queen, and they scarce slept at night for thinking of bright ribands and gay raiment.

But to Kriemhild more joyous than any hope of costly garments was the hope that at the great festival she would see, nay even speak with, her knight, Sir Siegfried.

Folded away in large chests Queen Uté had a store of rich raiment. Robes of white embroidered in gold, and sparkling with gems, she now brought forth, robes of purple and blue and many another colour she laid before the eyes of her bewildered maidens. These the Queen herself had worked through the glad days of summer, and through the dark winter evenings.

The festival was to be held at Whitsuntide, and as the time drew near, noble guests were seen daily riding into Worms. Kings came from afar, thirty-two princes also had journeyed thither, and when Whitsun morning dawned, five thousand men and more had come to Rhineland, where free from care dwelt King Gunther.

When the knights had entered the lists, the King sent a hundred of his liegemen that they might bring Queen Uté and her gentle daughter to the great hall.

Clad in their rich robes of state, the Queen and her many maidens came, and among them all was none to compare with the peerless maiden Kriemhild. When Siegfried saw the Princess he knew that she was indeed more radiant in her beauty than he had even dreamed, and the hero's heart grew heavy.

How could it ever be that he should wed so fair, so kind a maiden. He could see the kindness shining in her bright eyes. Yet surely he had but dreamed a foolish dream, and thinking thus the knight grew pale and troubled.

Then King Gernot, whose eyes saw what other eyes were ofttimes too dull to heed, then King Gernot, seeing Siegfried's cheeks grow pale, said to his brother Gunther, 'Bid the hero who hath served thee right nobly, bid him go greet our sister. For though she hath scorned full many a knight, him will she welcome with right good cheer.'

King Gernot's words pleased his royal brother, and a messenger was sent to Siegfried, bidding him greet the Princess.

Swift then leaped the roses to Sir Siegfried's cheeks, as he hastened to where Kriemhild sat among her maidens.

'Be welcome here, Sir Siegfried, for thou art a good and noble knight,' said the maiden softly. Then, as in reverence he bent low before his lady, she rose and took his right hand graciously in her own.

As they stood thus together the great bells of the Minster pealed, and lords and ladies wended their way to the church of God to hear a Mass sung, and to give thanks for the great victory the Burgundian heroes had won.

At the Minster door Siegfried must needs leave the Princess that she might sit among her maidens. But when the service was ended they walked together to the castle.

'Now God reward thee, Siegfried,' said the maiden, 'for right well hast thou served my royal brother.'

'Thee I will serve forever,' cried the happy hero, 'thee will I serve forever, and thy wishes shall ever be my will!'

Then for twelve glad days were Siegfried and Kriemhild ofttimes side by side. And when he tilted in the tournament, he felt that the bright eyes of his lady were shining upon him, and his skill was greater even than it had used to be. At length the merry Maytide games were over.

Gifts of gold and silks did King Gunther bestow on all his guests ere they set out for their own lands. Queen Uté also and the Princess wished them Godspeed as they filed slowly past the royal throne.

The festival was over, and it might be he would see the fair maiden Kriemhild no more, so thought the hero. Well, he would away, away to his own home in the Netherlands once more.

But Giselher, Kriemhild's youngest brother, heard that Siegfried was making ready to leave the royal city, and he begged him to stay.

'Tarry here a little longer,' he said, 'and each day, when toil or sport is over, thou shalt see my fair sister, Kriemhild.'

'Bid my steed be taken back to its stall,' then cried the happy knight, 'and hang my shield upon the wall.'

Thus in the gladsome summer days Siegfried and Kriemhild walked and talked together, and ever did the knight love the gentle maiden more.

CHAPTER IX
SIEGFRIED GOES TO ISENLAND

Whitsuntide had come and gone when tidings from beyond the Rhine reached the court at Worms.

No dread tidings were these, but glad and good to hear, of a matchless Queen named Brunhild who dwelt in Isenland. King Gunther listened with right goodwill to the tales of this warlike maiden, for if she were beautiful she was also strong as any warrior.

Wayward, too, she was, yet Gunther would fain have her as his queen to sit beside him on his throne.

One day the King sent for Siegfried to tell him that he would fain journey to Isenland to wed Queen Brunhild.

Now Siegfried, as you know, had been in Isenland and knew some of the customs of this wayward Queen. So he answered the King right gravely that it would be a dangerous journey across the sea to Isenland, nor would he win the Queen unless he were able to vanquish her great strength.

He told the King how Brunhild would challenge him to three contests or games, as she would call them. And if she were the victor, as indeed she had been over many a royal suitor, then his life would be forfeited.

At her own desire kings and princes had hurled the spear at the stalwart Queen, and it had but glanced harmless off her shield, while she would pierce the armour of these valiant knights with her first thrust. This was one of the Queen's games.

Then the knights would hasten to the ring and throw the stone from them as far as might be, yet ever Queen Brunhild threw it farther. For this was another game of the warrior Queen.

The third game was to leap beyond the stone which they had thrown, but ever to their dismay the knights saw this marvellous maiden far outleap them all. These valorous knights, thus beaten in the three contests, had been beheaded, and therefore it was that Siegfried spoke so gravely to King Gunther.

But Gunther, so he said, was willing to risk his life to win so brave a bride.

Now Hagen had drawn near to the King, and as he listened to Siegfried's words, the grim warrior said, 'Sire, since the Prince knows the customs of Isenland, let him go with thee on thy journey, to share thy dangers, and to aid thee in the presence of this warlike Queen.'

And Hagen, for he hated the hero, hoped that he might never return alive from Isenland. But the King was pleased with his counsellor's words. 'Sir Siegfried,' he said, 'wilt thou help me to win the matchless maiden Brunhild for my queen?'

'That right gladly will I do,' answered the Prince, 'if thou wilt promise to give to me thy sister Kriemhild as my bride, should I bring thee back safe from Isenland, the bold Queen at thy side.'

Then the King promised that on the same day that he wedded Brunhild, his sister should wed Prince Siegfried, and with this promise the hero was well content.

'Thirty thousand warriors will I summon to go with us to Isenland,' cried King Gunther gaily.

'Nay,' said the Prince, 'thy warriors would but be the victims of this haughty Queen. As plain knight-errants will we go, taking with us none, save Hagen the keen-eyed and his brother Dankwart.'

Then King Gunther, his face aglow with pleasure, went with Sir Siegfried to his sister's bower, and begged her to provide rich garments in which he and his knights might appear before the beauteous Queen Brunhild.

'Thou shalt not beg this service from me,' cried the gentle Princess, 'rather shalt thou command that which thou dost wish. See, here have I silk in plenty. Send thou the gems from off thy bucklers, and I and my maidens will work them with gold embroideries into the silk.'

Thus the sweet maiden dismissed her brother, and sending for her thirty maidens who were skilled in needlework she bade them sew their daintiest stitches, for here were robes to be made for the King and Sir Siegfried ere they went to bring Queen Brunhild into Rhineland.

For seven weeks Kriemhild and her maidens were busy in their bower. Silk white as new-fallen snow, silk green as the leaves in spring did they shape into garments worthy to be worn by the King and Sir Siegfried, and amid the gold embroideries glittered many a radiant gem.

Meanwhile down by the banks of the Rhine a vessel was being built to carry the King across the sea to Isenland.

When all was ready the King and Sir Siegfried went to the bower of the Princess. They would put on the silken robes and the beautiful cloaks Kriemhild and her maidens had sewed to see that they were neither too long nor too short. But indeed the skilful hands of the Princess had not erred. No more graceful or more beautiful garments had ever before been seen by the King or the Prince.

'Sir Siegfried,' said the gentle Kriemhild, 'care for my royal brother lest danger befall him in the bold Queen's country. Bring him home both safe and sound I beseech thee.'

The hero bowed his head and promised to shield the King from danger, then they said farewell to the maiden, and embarked in the little ship that awaited them on the banks of the Rhine. Nor did Siegfried forget to take with him his Cloak of Darkness and his good sword Balmung.

Now none was there on the ship save King Gunther, Siegfried, Hagen, and Dankwart, but Siegfried with his Cloak of Darkness had the strength of twelve men as well as his own strong right hand.

Merrily sailed the little ship, steered by Sir Siegfried himself. Soon the Rhine river was left behind and they were out on the sea, a strong wind filling their sails. Ere evening, full twenty miles had the good ship made.

For twelve days they sailed onward, until before them rose the grim fortress that guarded Isenland.

'What towers are these?' cried King Gunther, as he gazed upon the turreted castle which looked as a grim sentinel guarding the land.

'These,' answered the hero, 'are Queen Brunhild's towers and this is the country over which she rules.'

Then turning to Hagen and Dankwart Siegfried begged them to let him be spokesman to the Queen, for he knew her wayward moods. 'And King Gunther shall be my King,' said the Prince, 'and I but his vassal until we leave Isenland.'

And Hagan and Dankwart, proud men though they were, obeyed in all things the words of the young Prince of the Netherlands.

CHAPTER X
SIEGFRIED SUBDUES BRUNHILD

The little ship had sailed on now close beneath the castle, so close indeed that as the King looked up to the window he could catch glimpses of beautiful maidens passing to and fro.

Sir Siegfried also looked and laughed aloud for glee. It would be but a little while until Brunhild was won and he was free to return to his winsome lady Kriemhild.

By this time the maidens in the castle had caught sight of the ship, and many bright eyes were peering down upon King Gunther and his three brave comrades.

'Look well at the fair maidens, sire,' said Siegfried to the King. 'Among them all show me her whom thou wouldst choose most gladly as your bride.'

'Seest thou the fairest of the band,' cried the King, 'she who is clad in a white garment? It is she and no other whom I would wed.' Right merrily then laughed Siegfried. 'The maiden,' said he gaily, 'is in truth none other than Queen Brunhild herself.'

The King and his warriors now moored their vessel and leaped ashore, Siegfried leading with him the King's charger. For each knight had brought his steed with him from the fair land of Burgundy.

More bright than ever beamed the bright eyes of the ladies at the castle window. So fair, so gallant a knight never had they seen, thought the damsels as they gazed upon Sir Siegfried. And all the while King Gunther dreamed their glances were bent on no other than himself.

Siegfried held the noble steed until King Gunther had mounted, and this he did that Queen Brunhild might not know that he was the Prince of the Netherlands, owing service to no man. Then going back to the ship the hero brought his own horse to land, mounted, and rode with the King toward the castle gate.

King and Prince were clad alike. Their steeds as well as their garments were white as snow, their saddles were bedecked with jewels, and on the harness hung bells, all of bright red gold. Their shields shone as the sun, their spears they wore before them, their swords hung by their side.

Behind them followed Hagen and Dankwart, their armour black as the plumage of the wild raven, their shields strong and mighty.

As they approached the castle the gates were flung wide open, and the liegemen of the great Queen came out to greet the strangers with words of welcome. They bid their hirelings also take the shields and chargers from their guests.

But when a squire demanded that the strangers should also yield their swords, grim Hagen smiled his grimmest, and cried, 'Nay, our swords will we e'en keep lest we have need of them.' Nor was he too well pleased when Siegfried told him that the custom in Isenland was that no guest should enter the castle carrying a weapon. It was but sullenly that he let his sword be taken away along with his mighty shield.

After the strangers had been refreshed with wine, her liegemen sent to the Queen to tell her that strange guests had arrived.

'Who are the strangers who come thus unheralded to my land?' haughtily demanded Brunhild.

But no one could tell her who the warriors were, though some murmured that the tallest and fairest might be the great hero Siegfried.

It may be that the Queen thought that if the knight were indeed Siegfried she would revenge herself on him now for the mischievous pranks he had played the last time he was in her kingdom. In any case she said, 'If the hero is here he shall enter into contest with me, and he shall pay for his boldness with his life, for I shall be the victor.'

Then with five hundred warriors, each with his sword in hand, Brunhild came down to the knights from Burgundy.

'Be welcome, Siegfried,' she cried, 'yet wherefore hast thou come again to Isenland?'

'I thank thee for thy greeting, lady,' said the Prince 'but thou hast welcomed me before my lord. He, King Gunther, ruler over the fair realms of Burgundy, hath come hither to wed with thee.'

Brunhild was displeased that the mighty hero should not himself seek to win her as a bride, yet since for all his prowess he seemed but a vassal of the King, she answered, 'If thy master can vanquish me in the contests to which I bid him, then I will be his wife, but if I conquer thy master, his life, and the lives of his followers will be forfeited.'

'What dost thou demand of my master?' asked Hagen. 'He must hurl the spear with me, throw the stone from the ring, and leap to where it has fallen,' said the Queen.

Now while Brunhild was speaking, Siegfried whispered to the King to fear nothing, but to accept the Queen's challenge. 'I will be near though no one will see me, to aid thee in the struggle,' he whispered. Gunther had such trust in the Prince that he at once cried boldly, 'Queen Brunhild, I do not fear even to risk my life that I may win thee for my bride.'

Then the bold maiden called for her armour, but when Gunther saw her shield, ‹three spans thick with gold and iron, which four chamberlains could hardly bear,› his courage began to fail.

While the Queen donned her silken fighting doublet, which could turn aside the sharpest spear, Siegfried slipped away unnoticed to the ship, and swiftly flung around him his Cloak of Darkness. Then unseen by all, he hastened back to King Gunther's side.

A great javelin was then given to the Queen, and she began to fight with her suitor, and so hard were her thrusts that but for Siegfried the King would have lost his life. 'Give me thy shield,' whispered the invisible hero in the King's ear, 'and tell no one

The maiden hurled her spear.

that I am here.' Then as the maiden hurled her spear with all her force against the shield which she thought was held by the King, the shock well-nigh drove both Gunther and his unseen friend to their knees.

But in a moment Siegfried's hand had dealt the Queen such a blow with the handle of his spear (he would not use the sharp point against a woman) that the maiden cried aloud, 'King Gunther, thou hast won this fray.'

For as she could not see Siegfried because of his Cloak of Darkness, she could not but believe that it was the King who had vanquished her.

In her wrath the Queen now sped to the ring, where lay a stone so heavy that it could scarce be lifted by twelve strong men.

But Brunhild lifted it with ease, and threw it twelve arms' length beyond the spot on which she stood. Then, leaping after it, she alighted even farther than she had thrown the stone.

Gunther now stood in the ring, and lifted the stone which had again been placed within it. He lifted it with an effort, but at once Siegfried's unseen hand grasped it and threw it with such strength that it dropped even beyond the spot to which it had been flung by the Queen.

Lifting King Gunther with him Siegfried next jumped far beyond the spot on which the Queen had alighted. And all the warriors marvelled to see their Queen thus vanquished by the strange King. For you must remember that not one of them could see that it was Siegfried who had done these deeds of prowess.

Now in the contest, still unseen, Siegfried had taken from the Queen her ring and her favourite girdle.

With angry gestures Brunhild called to her liegemen to come and lay their weapons down at King Gunther's feet to do him homage. Henceforth they must be his thralls and own him as their lord.

As soon as the contests were over, Siegfried had slipped back to the ship and hidden his Cloak of Darkness. Then boldly he came back to the great hall, and pretending to know nothing of the games begged to be told who had been the victor, if indeed they had already taken place.

When he had heard that Queen Brunhild had been vanquished, the hero laughed, and cried gaily, 'Then, noble maiden, thou must go with us to Rhineland to wed King Gunther.'

'A strange way for a vassal to speak,' thought the angry Queen, and she answered with a proud glance at the knight, 'Nay, that will I not do until I have summoned my kinsmen and my good lieges. For I will myself say farewell to them ere ever I will go to Rhineland.'

Thus heralds were sent throughout Brunhild's realms, and soon from morn to eve her kinsmen and her liegemen rode into the castle, until it seemed as though a mighty army were assembling.

'Does the maiden mean to wage war against us,' said Hagen grimly. 'I like not the number of her warriors.'

Then said Siegfried, 'I will leave thee for a little while and go across the sea, and soon will I return with a thousand brave warriors, so that no evil may befall us.'

So the Prince went down alone to the little ship and set sail across the sea.

CHAPTER XI
SIEGFRIED GOES TO THE CAVE

The ship in which Siegfried set sail drifted on before the wind, while those in Queen Brunhild's castle marvelled, for no one was to be seen on board. This was because the

hero had again donned his Cloak of Darkness.

On and on sailed the little ship until at length it drew near to the land of the Nibelungs. Then Siegfried left his vessel and again climbed the mountainside, where long before he had cut off the heads of the little Nibelung princes.

He reached the cave into which he had thrust the treasure, and knocked loudly at the door. The cave was the entrance to Nibelheim the dark, little town beneath the glad, green grass.

Siegfried might have entered the cave, but he knocked that he might see if his treasure were well guarded.

Then the porter, who was a great giant, when he heard the knock buckled on his armour and opened the door. Seeing, as he thought in his haste, a strange knight standing before him he fell upon him with a bar of iron. So strong was the giant that it was with difficulty that the Prince overcame him and bound him hand and foot.

Alberich meanwhile had heard the mighty blows, which indeed had shaken Nibelheim to its foundations.

Now the dwarf had sworn fealty to Siegfried, and when he, as the giant had done, mistook the Prince for a stranger, he seized a heavy whip with a gold handle and rushed upon him, smiting his shield with the knotted whip until it fell to pieces.

Too pleased that his treasures were so well defended to be angry, Siegfried now seized the little dwarf by his beard, and pulled it so long and so hard that Alberich was forced to cry for mercy.

Then Siegfried bound him hand and foot as he had done the giant.

Alberich, poor little dwarf, gnashed his teeth with rage. Who would guard the treasure now, and who would warn his master that a strong man had found his way to Nibelheim?

But in the midst of his fears he heard the stranger's merry laugh. Nay, it was no stranger, none but the hero Prince could laugh thus merrily.

'I am Siegfried your master,' then said the Prince. 'I did but test thy faithfulness, Alberich,' and laughing still, the hero undid the cords with which he had bound the giant and the dwarf.

'Call me here quickly the Nibelung warriors,' cried Siegfried, 'for I have need of them.' And soon thirty thousand warriors stood before him in shining armour.

Choosing one thousand of the strongest and biggest, the Prince marched with them down to the seashore. There they embarked in ships and sailed away to Isenland.

Now it chanced that Queen Brunhild was walking on the terrace of her sea-guarded castle with King Gunther when she saw a number of sails approaching.

'Whose can these ships be?' she cried in quick alarm.

'These are my warriors who have followed me from Burgundy,' answered the King, for thus had Siegfried bidden him speak.

'We will go to welcome the fleet,' said Brunhild, and together they met the brave Nibelung army and lodged them in Isenland.

'Now will I give of my silver and my gold to my liegemen and to Gunther's warriors,' said Queen Brunhild, and she held out the keys of her treasury to Dankwart that he might do her will. But so lavishly did the knight bestow her gold and her costly gems and her rich raiment upon the warriors that the Queen grew angry.

'Nought shall I have left to take with me to Rhineland,' she cried aloud in her vexation.

'In Burgundy,' answered Hagen, 'there is gold enough and to spare. Thou wilt not need the treasures of Isenland.'

But these words did not content the Queen. She would certainly take at least twenty coffers of gold as well as jewels and silks with her to King Gunther's land.

At length, leaving Isenland to the care of her brother, Queen Brunhild, with twenty hundred of her own warriors as a body-guard, with eighty-six dames and one hundred maidens, set out for the royal city of Worms.

For nine days the great company journeyed homeward, and then King Gunther entreated Siegfried to be his herald to Worms. 'Beg Queen Uté and the Princess Kriemhild,' said the King, 'beg them to ride forth to meet my bride and to prepare to hold high festival in honour of the wedding feast.'

Thus Siegfried with four-and-twenty knights sailed on more swiftly than the other ships, and landing at the mouth of the river Rhine, rode hastily toward the royal city.

The Queen and her daughter, clad in their robes of state, re-ceived the hero, and his heart was glad, for once again he stood in the presence of his dear lady, Kriemhild.

'Be welcome, my Lord Siegfried,' she cried, 'thou worthy knight, be welcome. But where is my brother? Has he been van-quished by the warrior Queen? Oh, woe is me if he is lost, woe is me that ever I was born,' and the tears rolled down the maiden's cheeks.

'Nay, now,' said the Prince, 'thy brother is well and of good cheer. I have come, a herald of glad tidings. For even now the King is on his way to Worms, bringing with him his hard-won bride.' Then the Princess dried her tears, and graciously did she bid the hero to sit by her side.

'I would I might give thee a reward for thy services,' said the gentle maiden, 'but too rich art thou to receive my gold.'

'A gift from thy hands would gladden my heart,' said the gal-lant Prince. Blithely then did Kriemhild send for four-and-twenty buckles, all inlaid with precious stones, and these did she give to Siegfried.

Siegfried and the lady Kriemhild

Siegfried bent low before the lady Kriemhild, for well did he love the gracious giver, yet would he not keep for himself her gifts, but gave them, in his courtesy, to her four-and-twenty maidens.

Then the Prince told Queen Uté that the King begged her and the Princess to ride forth from Worms to greet his bride, and to prepare to hold high festival in the royal city.

'It shall be done even as the King desires,' said the Queen, while Kriemhild sat silent, smiling with gladness, because her knight Sir Siegfried had come home.

CHAPTER XII
THE WEDDING FEAST

In joy and merriment the days flew by, while the court at Worms prepared to hold high festival in honour of King Gunther's matchless bride.

As the royal ships drew near Queen Uté and the Princess Kriemhild, accompanied by many a gallant knight, rode along the banks of the Rhine to greet Queen Brunhild.

Already the King had disembarked, and was leading his bride toward his gracious mother. Courteously did Queen Uté welcome the stranger, while Kriemhild kissed her and clasped her in her arms. Some as they gazed upon the lovely maidens said that the warlike Queen Brunhild was more beautiful than the gentle Princess Kriemhild, but others, and these were the wiser, said that none could excel the peerless sister of the King.

In the great plain of Worms silk tents and gay pavilions had been placed. And there the ladies took shelter from the heat, while before them knights and warriors held a gay tournament. Then in the cool of the evening, a gallant train of lords and ladies, they rode toward the castle at Worms.

Queen Uté and her daughter went to their own apartments, while the King with Brunhild went into the banqueting hall where the wedding feast was spread.

But ere the feast had begun, Siegfried came and stood before the King.

'Sire,' he said, 'hast thou forgotten thy promise, that when Brunhild entered the royal city thy lady sister should be my bride?'

'Nay,' cried the King, 'my royal word do I ever keep,' and going out into the hall he sent for the Princess.

'Dear sister,' said Gunther, as she bowed before him, 'I have pledged my word to a warrior that thou wilt become his bride, wilt thou help me to keep my promise?'

Now Siegfried was standing by the King's side as he spoke.

Then the gentle maiden answered meekly, 'Thy will, dear brother, is ever mine. I will take as lord him to whom thou hast promised my hand.'

And she glanced shyly at Siegfried, for surely this was the warrior to whom her royal brother had pledged his word.

Right glad then was the King, and Siegfried grew rosy with delight as he received the lady's troth. Then together they went to the banqueting hall, and on a throne next to King Gunther sat the hero-prince, the lady Kriemhild by his side.

But when Brunhild saw the King's beautiful sister sitting on a throne with Siegfried by her side, she began to weep.

'Why dost thou weep, fair lady?' said King Gunther. 'Are not my lands, my castles, and all my warriors thine? Dim not thy bright eyes with thy tears.'

'I may well weep,' said Queen Brunhild, 'because thy sister has plighted her troth to one who is but a vassal of thine own. Thy sister is worthy of a prince.'

'Weep not,' cried the King, 'and when the banquet is ended I will tell thee how it is that Siegfried has won the hand of my lady sister.'

'Nay,' cried the impatient Queen, 'thou must tell me without delay or never will I be thy wife,' and Brunhild arose and stepped down from the throne.

King Gunther was displeased with the Queen's impatience, yet lest his guests should be disturbed, he answered her quickly:

'The hero Siegfried has as many castles as have I, and his realms are broader. In truth he is no vassal of mine. Ere long he will be King of the Netherlands.' Brunhild could but hide her anger now, yet in her heart she disliked Siegfried more than she had done before. It did not please her that he should be a greater king than Gunther.

When the banquet was ended, the wedding was celebrated, and the King placed a crown upon the brow of the haughty bride, for now she was his wife, and Queen of his fair realm of Burgundy.

Siegfried too was wedded to the maiden whom he loved so well, and though he had no crown to place upon her brow, the Princess was well content.

As wedding gifts the hero gave to his dear wife the treasure he had won from the Nibelungs, also the girdle and the ring which he had taken from Brunhild in her contests with King Gunther.

With his merry laugh Siegfried told his wife how he had fought for her royal brother, himself unseen, because he had on his Cloak of Darkness. And Kriemhild listening thought never had she known so fair, so brave a knight.

For fourteen days the wedding festivities never ceased. Then King Gunther and Prince Siegfried scattered costly gifts among their guests, so that they returned to their own lands in great glee.

No sooner were the guests departed than Siegfried also began to make ready to journey to his own country. Fain would he take his beautiful wife to see Siegmund and Sieglinde, and to dwell in the land over which one day he would be king.

Kriemhild, too, was glad to go to her dear lord's country. Taking a loving farewell of her lady mother, Queen Uté, and of her royal brothers, with five hundred knights of Burgundy and thirty-two Burgundian maids, Kriemhild rode away, Sir Siegfried by her side.

CHAPTER XIII
SIEGFRIED GOES HOME WITH KRIEMHILD

In the court of the Netherlands there was great gladness, for tidings had come that Prince Siegfried and his beautiful wife were already on their homeward way.

King Siegmund rejoiced, and resolved that now indeed his

son should wear the crown. Sieglinde wept for joy, then dried her tears, and bade her maidens look out their richest robes that they might welcome the young bride as became her rank.

Then the King and Queen rode forth to meet the travellers, and greeted them with kisses and fair words, and with great rejoicings the whole company returned to the castle. Here a great feast was held, and Siegmund, calling together all his liegemen, placed the crown upon his dear son's head, bidding them henceforth swear fealty to him alone.

The Netherlanders were indeed well pleased to have the mighty hero Siegfried for their king, and the castle walls shook with the shouts of strong men crying, 'Hail, King Siegfried, hail!'

For ten years Siegfried ruled and did justice in the land. At the end of ten years a little son came to gladden the hearts of the brave King and his gentle wife, and in memory of her royal brother, Kriemhild named him Gunther.

Now Queen Sieglinde had grown old and feeble, and after her little grandson had been born she grew still more weak until one day she passed away from earth.

Then Kriemhild took charge of the royal household. So kind was she and gentle that she was loved by all her maidens and indeed by all who dwelt in the castle.

Meanwhile Brunhild, the haughty Queen of Burgundy, was not happy, even her little son could not bring joy to her heart. Little had she to vex her, yet day by day her unhappiness grew.

Siegfried was now a mightier King than Gunther, and this displeased her more and more, for certainly he had once been but her lord's vassal.

Had she not herself, from her castle window at Isenland, seen him hold King Gunther's charger until he had mounted, and that a Prince would have scorned to do. Yet today Siegfried was a King, Brunhild could not understand how this could be, and the more she thought about it, the angrier she grew. Even the gentle Kriemhild seemed to have grown haughty and disdainful, and for her too Brunhild had no love.

At length Brunhild made up her mind to speak to her husband.

'It is many years,' she said to King Gunther, 'since Siegfried has been at Worms. Bid him come hither with his wife.'

Then Gunther frowned, ill-pleased at her words. 'Thou dost not dream that I may command so mighty a King as Siegfried!' he cried.

But these words only made the Queen more angry. 'However great Siegfried may be, he dare not disobey his lord,' she said.

King Gunther smiled to himself at Brunhild's foolish thoughts. Full well he knew that the King of the Netherlands owed no duty to him, the King of Burgundy.

Then Brunhild, seeing that by anger she would not gain her wish, smiled and coming close to Gunther said, 'My lord, fain would I see thy sweet sister once more. If thou mayest not bid, wilt thou not entreat Siegfried to bring Kriemhild to our country that again we may sit together as we were used to do? In truth the gentleness of thy lady sister did ever please me well.'

Now Gunther, hearing his wife's kind words, was wishful to do her will. Therefore he sent for thirty warriors, and bade them ride into King Siegfried's land, and entreat him once again to come with his fair wife to the royal city of Worms. Queen Uté also sent messages to Queen Kriemhild beseeching her to come again to her own country.

Well pleased was Kriemhild when the knights from Burgundy were shown into her presence, and right glad was the welcome given to them by King Siegfried. Then one of the knights hastened to deliver King Gunther's greetings and the greetings of Queen Uté and her ladies.

'The King and Queen bid you also welcome to a high festival which they hold as soon as the winter is ended,' he said.

But King Siegfried, thinking of all the business of the state, answered courteously, 'Nay, I fear that I may scarce leave my land without a king. Yet will I lodge you here while I take counsel with my liegemen.'

For nine days King Gunther's men tarried in the Netherlands, and banquets and tournaments were given in their honour.

Then Siegfried summoned his liegemen together and told them of King Gunther's desire that he and his Queen should go to Rhineland, and bade them give him their counsel.

'Take with thee a thousand warriors, sire, and if it be thy will ride thus into Burgundy,' said the King's chief adviser.

'I also will go with thee,' said Siegmund, for well did he love his son. 'I also will go with thee and take a hundred swordsmen along with me.'

Right glad was Siegfried when he heard his father's words. 'My own good father dear,' he cried, and seizing his hand he kissed it. 'In twelve days will I leave my realm and journey toward Burgundy, and thou shalt ride with me and Queen Kriemhild.'

Then the heralds of King Gunther, laden with rich gifts, were bidden to hasten back to their own land with tidings that Siegfried and his Queen would ere long follow them to the royal city.

When the heralds stood again before King Gunther, they delivered their tidings, and then spread out before him and his courtiers the raiment and the gold which Siegfried had bestowed upon them.

Hagen looked upon the gifts, his keen eyes full of greed. 'Well may the mighty King Siegfried give such gifts,' he said. 'If he were to live for ever, yet could he not spend the great treasure which he possesses in the land of the Nibelungs.'

CHAPTER XIV
SIEGFRIED AND KRIEMHILD
GO TO WORMS

One fine morning Siegfried and all his fair company set out on their journey to Rhineland. Their little son they left at the palace in the Netherlands.

As they drew near to Burgundy, a band of Gunther's most gallant warriors rode forth to meet their guests. Brunhild also went to greet the royal company, yet in her heart the hatred she felt for Siegfried and his wife grew ever more fierce, more cruel.

Gunther rejoiced when he saw the brave lighthearted hero once again, and he welcomed him right royally. As for Brunhild, she kissed the Queen of the Netherlands, and smiled upon her, so that the lovely lady was well pleased with her greeting.

Twelve hundred gallant warriors sat round the banqueting table in the good city of Worms that day. Then the feast ended, and the travellers sought their couches, weary with their long journey. The next morning the great chests which they had brought with them were opened, and many precious stones, and many beautiful garments were bestowed by King Siegfried and Queen Kriemhild on the ladies and the knights of the royal city.

Queen Uté, too, was happy, for now again she might look upon the face of her dear daughter.

Then a tournament was held, and the knights tilted, while beautiful damsels looked down upon them from the galleries of the great hall. And at evensong the happy court would wend its way to the Minster, and there, the Queens, wearing their crowns of state, would enter side by side. Thus for eleven days all went merry as a marriage ball.

One evening, ere the Minster bell pealed for vespers, the two Queens sat side by side under a silken tent. They were talking of Siegfried and Gunther, their lords.

'There is no braver warrior in the wide world than my lord Siegfried,' said Kriemhild.

'Nay,' cried Brunhild angrily, 'nay, thou dost forget thy brother, King Gunther. None, I trow, is mightier than he.'

Then the gentle Kriemhild forgot her gentle ways, and bitter to Queen Brunhild's ears were the words she spoke.

'My royal brother is neither strong nor brave as is my lord,' she cried. 'Dost thou not know that Siegfried it was, not Gunther, who vanquished thee in the contests held at thy castle in Isenland? Dost thou not know that it was Siegfried, clad in his Coat of Darkness, who wrested from thee both thy girdle and thy ring?' And Kriemhild pointed to the girdle which she was wearing round her waist, to the ring which she was wearing on her finger.

Brunhild, when she saw her girdle and her ring, wept, and her tears were tears of anger. Never would she forgive Siegfried for treating her thus; never would she forgive Kriemhild for telling her the truth.

'Alas! alas!' cried the angry Queen, 'no hero have I wed, but a feeble-hearted knave.'

Meanwhile, Kriemhild, already grieved that she had spoken thus foolishly, had left the angry Queen and gone down to the Minster to vespers.

That evening Brunhild had no smiles, no gentle words, for her lord.

'It was Siegfried, not thou, my lord, who vanquished me in the contests at Isenland,' she said in a cold voice to the startled King.

Had Siegfried then dared to boast to the Queen of the wonderful feats he had done in the land across the sea? Nay, King Gunther could not quite believe that the hero would thus boast of his great strength.

But the Queen was still scolding him, so Gunther, in his dismay, stammered, 'We will summon the King to our presence, and he shall tell us why he has dared to boast of his might as though he were stronger than I.'

When Siegfried stood before the angry Brunhild, the crestfallen King said as sternly as he dared, 'Hast thou boasted that it was thou who conquered the maiden Brunhild?'

But even as he spoke all Gunther's suspicions fled away. Siegfried with the steadfast eyes and the happy laugh had never betrayed him. Of that he felt quite sure. It was true that he might have told his wife Kriemhild——

Ah, now King Gunther knew what had happened! Not Siegfried, but his lady sister had told Brunhild the secret. Truly it was no fault of the gallant hero that Queen Brunhild had that day learned the secret which he would fain have kept from her for ever.

So King Gunther stretched out his hand to Siegfried, who had stood in silence before him, and said, 'Not thou, but my sister Kriemhild hath boasted of thy prowess in Isenland,' and the two Kings walked away together leaving Brunhild in her anger.

But not long was she left to weep alone, for Hagen, the keen-eyed, coming into the hall, saw her tears.

'Gracious lady, wherefore dost thou weep?' he asked. 'I weep for anger,' said Brunhild, and she told Hagen the foolish words which Siegfried's wife had spoken.

When Hagen had heard them he smiled grimly to himself. Siegfried, the hero, nor his beautiful wife, should escape his vengeance now. And he began at once to plan with the Queen how he might punish them. Well did he know that Brunhild would do all in her power to aid him in his plots.

Slowly but very surely Hagen drew Gernot and one or two warriors into his schemes against the King of the Netherlands.

But when Giselher heard that the cruel counsellors even wished to slay Siegfried, he was angry, and said bravely, 'Never has Siegfried deserved such hate from any knight of Burgundy.'

But Hagen did not cease his evil whispers against the hero. He would even steal upon King Gunther as he sat at his council-table, and he would whisper in his ear that if Siegfried were not so strong, his Burgundian heroes would win more glory for their arms, that if Siegfried were not living, all his broad lands would belong, through Kriemhild, to Burgundy.

At first, Gunther would bid Hagen be silent, and lay aside his hate of the mighty hero. But afterward he would listen and only murmur, 'If Siegfried heard thy words, none of us would be safe from his wrath.' For King Gunther was weak and easily made to fear.

'Fear not,' said Hagen grimly, 'Siegfried shall never hear of our plots. Leave the matter to me. I will send for two strange heralds to come to our land. They shall pretend that they have come from our old enemies, Ludegast and Ludeger, and they shall challenge us to battle once again.'

'When Siegfried hears that thou must go forth to fight, he will even as afore-time offer to go for thee against the foe. Then, methinks, shall I learn the secret of the great warrior's strength from Kriemhild, ere he set out, as she will believe he must do, for the battlefield.'

And Gunther listened and feared to gainsay the words of his wicked counsellor, also he thought of the great treasure, and longed that he might possess it.

CHAPTER XV
SIEGFRIED IS SLAIN

Hagen did not delay to carry out his wicked plot. Four days later, thirty-two strangers rode into Rhineland, and demanded to see King Gunther. These were the

men who had been hired by the counsellor to bring false tidings of battle.

When the heralds stood before the King their spokesman said, 'We come from King Ludegast and King Ludeger, who have gathered together new armies with which to invade thy land, and forthwith they challenge thee to combat.'

Then the King pretended that he did not know that these were false heralds with false tidings. He frowned, and his eyes flashed anger at the strangers as he listened to their words.

Siegfried, who had heard the strangers' words, cried eagerly, 'Fear not, O King, I and my warriors will fight for thee, even as afore-time we have done.'

Well pleased then seemed Gunther at the hero's words. As though he really feared the armies of the foreign kings, he graciously thanked Siegfried for his offered aid.

Gaily then did Siegfried summon his thousand warriors and bade them polish their armour and make their shields shine, for they must go forth to fight for the realm of Burgundy.

'Now,' thought Hagen, 'is the moment to win from Kriemhild the secret of her lord's strength,' so he hastened to her apartments to bid her farewell. For he, too, was going forth to battle.

When Kriemhild saw the grim warrior she cried, 'If thou art near to my lord in the battlefield, guard him for my sake, and ever shalt thou have Queen Kriemhild's thanks.'

'Right gladly will I serve Siegfried for thy sake,' said the false knight. 'Tell me how best I may guard thy lord.'

'Thou art my kinsman, Hagen,' said the noble lady, 'therefore will I trust thee with the secret of his strength.'

Then the Queen told the warrior of the tiny spot between her husband's shoulders on which the linden leaf had fallen while he bathed in the dragon's blood, and how, while all the rest of his body was too tough to be pierced by spear or arrow, on that spot, he might be wounded as easily as any other man.

Hagen's eyes glittered. The life of the King was well-nigh in his hands.

'If this be so, noble lady, I beg of thee sew a token upon his garment, that I may know the spot which I must guard with my shield, and if need be with my life,' said the counsellor.

Then Kriemhild promised to sew a tiny cross upon Siegfried's tunic, that so Hagen might the better be able to shield her lord.

Bowing low, Hagen said farewell, then hastened from the presence of the gentle lady whose trust he meant to betray and that right cruelly.

The next morning Siegfried set out, merrily as was his wont, at the head of his warriors, and close behind him rode Hagen, his keen eyes searching for the little cross.

It was there, the token which the lady Kriemhild had sewn with eager hands on her lord's tunic, thinking thus to guard him from all harm.

There was no need now for the pretence of war, for Hagen himself held Siegfried's life in his hands. The wicked counsellor, therefore, ordered two of his own followers to ride away in secret, bidding them return in a day or two, travel-stained, as though they had come from afar.

With them they were to bring tidings of submission and peace from Ludegast and Ludeger. Thus, before Siegfried and his great host had marched into the enemy's land they were stayed by heralds who brought messages of peace and goodwill to Gunther, and much against his wish the gallant hero had to return to Worms, no battle fought, no enemy conquered.

But if Siegfried grieved, Kriemhild rejoiced at his return. Already she had begun to be sorry that she had trusted her kinsman, Hagen.

Gunther, too, seemed happy to welcome Siegfried. 'Now that there is peace we will go a-hunting,' he said to the hero. Now this hunt had been planned by Hagen.

Then Siegfried went to say farewell to his beautiful wife ere he rode away to the hunt. But Kriemhild clung to him, begging her dear lord not to leave her. She longed to warn him, too, against Hagen, yet this she did not dare to do.

'Ah, my lord,' she cried, 'last night I dreamed that two wild boars chased thee, and again I dreamed that as thou didst ride into the valley two mountains fell upon thee and hid thee forever from my sight. Go not to the hunt, my dear lord Siegfried.'

Yet the hero would not heed the dreams of his lady. Gently he loosened her hands, and saying farewell, he left her weeping.

Out in the glad sunshine Siegfried smiled. He would be back so soon to comfort his dear wife, and then she, too, would laugh at her fears, and thinking thus he joined Gunther and his merry huntsmen, and together they rode toward the forest.

Never had there been such a hunt or such merry huntsmen, and no prey seemed to escape the hero Siegfried.

A strong and savage ox he felled to the ground with his own hand. A lion sprang toward him, but swiftly the hero drew his bow, and it lay harmless at his feet. An elk, a buffalo, four strong bisons, a fierce stag, and many a hart and hind were slain by his prowess. But when, with his sword, he slew a wild boar that had attacked him, his comrades slipped the leash round the hounds and cried, 'Lord Siegfried, nought is there left alive in the forest. Let us return to the camp with our spoils.'

At that moment, clear and loud rang out the hunting horn. It was the King who bade it sound that his merry huntsmen might come to feast with him in the green meadow on the outskirts of the forest.

Now the horn had roused a grisly bear, and Siegfried, seeing it, jumped from his charger, chased it, and having at length caught it with his strong right hand, bound it without receiving even a scratch from its claws or a bite from its jaws.

Then the hero dragged the bear back to his charger, tied it to his saddle, and mounting rode quickly forward to the camp.

King Gunther watched him as he drew near, and so gallant and brave he looked, that his heart grew heavy because he had listened to the cruel counsels of his uncle Hagen.

The hero wore a tunic of black velvet, a riding cap of sable. By his side hung his good sword Balmung, a quiver thrust through his girdle was filled with arrows, the shafts of which were golden.

Before he reached the camp, Siegfried again alighted and loosed the great bear, and bewildered, the brute sprang forward into the camp kitchen.

Up sprang the scullions from the fire, kettles were toppled over, the fire was put out, fish, fowl, meat, all lay in the black and smoking ashes.

Then Gunther and his merry huntsmen chased the huge bear into the wood, and while all were swift, none was so swift as Siegfried. His good sword Balmung flashed in the air, and the bear was slain and carried back to the camp.

Now Hagen had arranged the feast for the huntsmen, and for his own purpose he had ordered no wine.

'Where are the cupbearers?' cried Siegfried, who was thirsty after the day's sport.

'They have gone across the Rhine whither they thought we hunted,' said Hagen, the false knight. 'But there is a spring of cold water a little way off, thither may we go to quench our thirst.'

Siegfried soon rose to go to the fountain. Then Hagen drew near and said, 'Ofttimes I have heard that thou art sure and swift of foot. Wilt thou race with me to the spring?'

'If thou art at the fountain before me,' said the mighty hero, 'I will even lay myself at thy feet.'

Gunther heard Siegfried's words and shuddered. Yet now he dared not save the hero from his foe.

'I will bear my spear, my sword, my quiver, and my shield as I race,' said Siegfried. But Hagen and King Gunther, who also wished to run, stripped off their upper garments, that they might run more lightly.

Fleet of foot were Hagen and the King, yet fleeter still was Siegfried. He reached the well, loosened his sword, and laid it with his bow and arrows on the ground, and leant his spear against a linden tree that grew close to the fountain.

He looked down into the spring, yet though his thirst was great, so courteous was he that he would not drink before King Gunther. When Gunther reached the well, he knelt at once to drink, then having quenched his thirst he turned and wandered back along the hillside toward his merry huntsmen.

As Siegfried now bent over the spring, Hagen with stealthy steps crept near and drew the hero's sword and quiver out of his reach. Stealthy still, he seized the spear which rested against the linden tree. Then while Siegfried drank of the cool, clear water, Hagen stabbed him, straight through the little cross of silk which Kriemhild's gentle hand had sewed, he stabbed.

The cruel deed was done, and Hagen turned to flee, leaving the spear there where he had thrust it, between the hero's shoulders, where once, alas! had lain a linden leaf.

Siegfried sprang to his feet as he felt the cruel blow, and reached for his quiver that he might speed the traitor to his death, but neither quiver nor sword could he find.

Then unarmed save for his shield the wounded hero ran, nor could Hagen escape him. With his shield Siegfried struck the false knight such heavy blows that the precious stones dropped out of the shield and were scattered, and Hagen lay helpless at King Siegfried's feet.

Hagen stabs Siegfried

But Siegfried had no sword with which to slay his enemy, moreover his wound began to smart until he writhed with pain.

Then, his strength failing him, he fell upon the green grass, while around him gathered Gunther and his huntsmen.

Sore wounded was King Siegfried, even unto death, and Gunther, sorry now the cruel deed was done, wept as he looked down upon the stricken King.

'Never would I have been slain, save by treachery,' murmured Siegfried. 'Yet how can I think of aught but my beautiful wife Kriemhild. Unto thee, O King Gunther, do I entrust her. If there be any faith in thee, defend her from all her foes.'

No more could he say, for he was faint from his wound, and ere long the hero lay still on the grass, dead. Then the knights, when they saw that the mighty King no longer breathed, laid him on a shield of gold, and when night fell they carried him thus, back to the royal city.

When Kriemhild knew that her lord, King Siegfried, was dead, bitter were her tears. Full well did she know that it was Hagen who had slain him, and greatly did she bemoan her foolishness in telling the grim counsellor the secret known to her alone.

The body of the great hero was laid in a coffin of gold and silver and carried to the Minster. Then when the days of mourning were over, the old King Siegmund and his warriors went sadly back to the Netherlands.

But Kriemhild stayed at Worms, and for thirteen years she mourned the loss of her dear lord.

Her sufferings, during these years, were made the greater through the greed of Hagen. For at the cruel warrior's bidding, Gunther went to the Queen and urged her to send for the treasure of the Nibelungs.

'It shall be guarded for thy use in the royal city,' said the King. In her grief Kriemhild cared little where the treasure was kept; and seeing this, her brother sent in her name to command that it should be brought to Worms.

No sooner, however, did it reach the city than it was seized upon by Hagen the traitor, and Kriemhild's wealth was no longer her own.

That henceforth it might be secure from every one save himself and King Gunther, Hagen buried the great treasure beneath the fast-flowing river Rhine.

When thirteen years had passed away, Kriemhild married Etzel, the powerful King of the Huns, and then at last Hagen began to fear. Would the lady to whom he had been so false punish him now that she was again a mighty Queen?

The years passed by, and Hagen was beginning to forget his fears when heralds came from Etzel, the King of the Huns, bidding King Gunther and his knights come visit Queen Kriemhild in her distant home. The command of Etzel was obeyed.

But no sooner did Hagen stand before her throne than Kriemhild commanded him to give her back the hidden treasure. This the grim counsellor refused to do.

'Then shalt not thou nor any of thy company return to Burgundy,' cried Kriemhild.

And as the Queen said, so it was, for the warriors of King Etzel fought with the warriors of King Gunther, until after a grievous slaughter not one Burgundian was left alive. Thus after many years was King Siegfried's death avenged by Queen Kriemhild.